anithmee Danji Danko Danna D... ...ny Dante Da... ...Da... Daiquiri
aragh Darby Darcey Darian Da... ...Dash Da... ...Davey
David Davina Dawsey Dawson Dax... ...Deanna De... ...De... Deborah
eclan Deekan Deeya Defne De... ...Dellza Delphi Delphina Delphine
elyn Demi Demilee Dennis Denny Derrick Derry Derya Deryn Destiny Dev Devina Devlin Devon
ewar Dexter Dhanya Dhillion Diana Dianne Diego Digby Digger Dillon Dilly Dilys Dima Dimitri
ina Dion Dix Dixie Diyari Dobby Doc Doireann Dolcie Dom Dominic Dominique Don Donald
onnacha Donovan Doone Dora Dorcas Dorian Dorota Dotty Doug Dougie Douglas Dov Dovid
rake Drew Drummond Dua Duff Duke Dulcie Duncan Duru Dusty Dyansa Dylan Eamonn
arn Easan Eban Ebba Ebby Ebony Echo Ed Eda
ddie Eden Edgar Edie Edina Edine Edison Edita
dith Ediz Edmund Edo Edona Edson Eduardo
dward Edwin Edwina Eesha Efa Efan Effia
ffie Egan Eide Eiko Eila Eilidh Eilis Eimear Eira
ire Eirini Eirlys Ei... Eirys Eisley Eitan
katerina Ekim Elaine Elan Elana
lara Elaria Eldon Eleana Eleanor
lectra E... Eleri Elfie Elia Eliana
lias F... Elili Elina Elinor Elio
lior... Elisia Elissa Elissia Eliza
l... Ellen Ellia Elliana Ellie
... Ella Ellison Ellora Ellouise
... Ellis Elouisa Elsa Elsabeth
...a Eloise Elora

My name is

... Elsia Elsie Elska Eluned Elva Elvie Elvis Elwin Elwood Elyan Elza Ember Emelia Emer
...ra Emerson Emi Emiko Emil Emilia Emiliana Emiliano Emilienne Emilio Emily Emin Emir
mira Emlyn Emma Emmalynn Emmanuel Emmanuelle Emme Emmeline Emmylou Emrys
na Endaf Endre Eneir Eneko Eni Enid Enna Ennio Ennis Enno Enola Enya Enys Enzo Eobha
oghan Ephraim Eponine Eray... Erica Erin Eriska Erlina Ernest Ernie Erva Eryithsyai Erykah
sa Eshan Esk Esma Esme E... ...da Espe Essa Essie Estella Estelle Esther Etan Etana Ethan
thel Ethenia Ether Et... ...Etienne Etta Ettie Euan Eugenia Euphemia Eva Evabelle
vadne Evaleigh Evan Evander Evangeli Evangelina Evangeline Eve Evelina Evelyn Everley
verlyn Evie Evive Evvie Evyatar Ewan Ewart Ewoo Ezekiel Ezmee Ezra Fabian Fabio Fable Fabrizio
aeryn Fairouz Faith Faizah Fallyn Fareed Farida Faris Farley Farooqi Farrah Farrell Farryn
atimah Fausta Faye Fayetastic Fedele Felicity Felix Fenella Fenia Fenn Fenya Feral Ferdi Ferdia
erelith Fergal Fergus Feronia Festa Ffion Fi Fia Fidela Fidelma Fifi Figgie Filomena Finan Finden
ndlay Finlaggan Finley Finlo Finn Finnbarr Finnian Fintan Finty Fiona Fionn Fionnuala Fitzroy
zz Fjord Flaminia Flavia Fletcher Fleur Flint Fliss Flo Floelyn Flora Florence Florentia Flori
orian Florrie Flossie Floyd Flynn Foma Fontan Fonzie Forbes Ford Fox Fran Frances Francesca
ancesco Franci Francis Franco Francois Frank Frankie Franklin Frannie Fraser Frasier Freddie
rederick Frederico Freya Friedrich Fuaad Fulco Funbunch Furkan Fyfe Gabe Gabin Gabriel
abriella Gabrielle Gaby Gage Gaia Gail Gaja Gal Gan Ganesh Garance Garbhán Gareth Garrett
avin Geir Gem Gemma Gene Geneva Genevieve Genie Geno Geoff Geordie George Georgette
eorgia Georgiana Georgie Georgina Gera Gerard Geri Germaine Gerti Gethin Ghalil Ghillie Gia

Giacomo Gideon Gigi Gil Gilad Gilbert Gillan Gina Ginevra Ginger Gino Giovana Giovanni Girma Gisell
Giselle Gladys Glen Glib Gloria Gloriana Gordon Gordy Grace Gracie Graciela Graham Grainn
Grant Graysie Grayson Greer Gregor Gregory Greig Greta Gretchen Gretel Griff Griffin Gruffyd
Gryffri Guillermo Gur Gurpreet Gus Gussie Guy Gwen Gwendolyn Gwennan Gwilym Gwyn Gwynet.
Gwynnie Gyöngyöske Haajaar Habiba Haddy Hadleigh Hadrien Haf Hag Haidee Hajra Haku Ha
Hali Halim Hallie Halo Hamda Hamilton Hamish Hamza Hanaan Hanahazala Hani Hani
Hank Hanley Hannah Hanxi Hanya Harley Harlow Harlyn Harman Harmony Haroon Harpe
Harriet Harris Harrison Harrold Harry Harshaan Harshita Haruki Haruma Harvey Hassa
Hattie Havana Haya Haydn Hayley Hazel Hazey Heaney Heath Heather Hebba Hebe Heck
Hector Hedwig Hedy Heeheon Heidi Helen Helena Hellie Héloïse Hendrik Hendrix Hendry Henle
Henna Henri Henrik Henry Herbert Herbie Heritage Hermione Hero Hester Hettie Hezekia
Hikari Hila Hiroki Holden Hollis Hollyanne Honesty Honor Honora Hope Horatio Hortense Howar
Howarth Howie Hozana Hubert Huckleberry Hudson Huey Hugh Hugo Humayra Humphre
Hunny Hunter Huon Huw Hux Huxley Hyehyeib Hyehyon Hyland Iago Ian Ianthe Iarla Ib Ibrahim
Icaro Ida Idahlia Idris Ifan Iga Iggi Ihita Ila Ilana Ilaria Iliana Ilona Ilsa Ilse Imala Immie Imoge
Imran Ina Inara Inayah Inca Indi India Indiana Indigo Indira Indrena Indus Ines Inessa Infinit
Ingrid Inidara Inigo Inishta Innes Io Iola Iolanthe Iolo Iona Ira Irene Iris Irvine Irving Isa Isaac Isabell
Isabelle Isadora Isaiah Isalind Isam Isamaya Ischia Isha Isiah Ishvar Isis Isla Islay Isle Ism
Isobel Isolde Issac Issy Iva Ivanka Ivo Ivor Iwan Iwona Izabelle Izel Izumi Izzie Jac Jack Jacki
Jackson Jacob Jacques Jacy Jad Jada Jadiel Jadina Jae Jafan Jago Jagraj Jai Jaim
Jaka Jake Jameela James Jamesina Jamie Jamieson Jan Jane Janie Jannah Janson Jan
Jardine Jared Jarrett Jarvis Jas Jasmina Jasmine Jasminka Jason Jasper Javier Jawari
Jaya Jayani Jayce Jaycee Jayda Jayden Jaydee Jayson Jazper Jean Jeanette Jeanin
Jeannie Jeb Jed Jeevan Jeffrey Jeja Jelena Jem Jemima Jemini Jemma Jen Jenn
Jennia Jennifer Jennita Jenny Jenson Jeremiah Jeremy Jerome Jerry Jersey Jesper Jes
Jessamy Jesse Jessica Jessie Jevon Jewel Jex Jez Ji-Hyun Jim Jimbo Jimi Jimmy Jing-We
Jio Jiya Jo Joan------------------quin Joban Jocelyn Jodie Joe Joel Joelle Joely Joe
Johanna John Johnny Jo------Jon Jonah Jonathan Joni Jonno Jonty Jools Jorda
Jorden Jordi Jorge---------Joseph Josephine Josh Joshua Josiah Josie Josip
Joss Josse Jouma----------Joyce Juan Judah Jude Judith Jules Julia Julia
Julianna Julian--------lius Julka Junayna Junie Junior Juniper Juno Junu
Jupiter Jura Ju----------Jusuf Jusveen Juul Kaan Kabir Kacey Kade Kade
Kady Kaela Kae----------ra Kairav Kako Kaleb Kaleeya Kali Kalia Kalina Kalli
Kallum Kalya Kamal Kami Kamilah Kamille Kamron Kana Kane Kani Kara Karaleig
Karam Karanpreet Kareena Karen Karenza Kari Karim Karimah Karina Karis Karishm
Karline Karlo Karly Karolina Karsen Karter Kashvi Kasia Kasmina Kasper Kat Katalina Katan
Katarina Kate Katharina Katharine Kathryn Kathy Katie Katinka Katla Katlin Katri
Katrina Katrine Katriona Katya Kava Kaya Kayaan Kayci Kayli Kaz Kaz
Keagan Kealan Keane Keaton Keegan Keelan Keely Keemia Keeva Keir Keira Keish
Keita KeKe Kellan Kelly Kelsey Kelynn Kemaya Ken Kenai Kenara Kendall Kendra Kenn
Kennedy Kenneth Kennise Kennosuke Kenny Keno Kensa Kensi Kenza Kenzie Kenzo Keo
Kepa Kerala Kerr Kerry Kerryn Kerys Keshav Ketan Kevin Keya Kezia Khalid Khalifa Khal
Khem Khloe Khunpol Khush Kia Kian Kiana Kiara Kieran Kierra Kieva Kievan Kiki Kikko Killia

JULIA DONALDSON'S
BOOK OF NAMES

Illustrated by
NILA AYE

MACMILLAN CHILDREN'S BOOKS

Do you need to find a name to give a girl or boy,
Or a puppy or a kitten, or a teddy or a toy?

Well, I've been signing children's books
for years and years and years,
And I've kept a list of names,
which might give you some ideas . . .

I've signed for Pearl and Ruby,
for Sapphire and for Jade,

JULIA DONALDSON'S
BOOK
OF
NAMES

Illustrated by
NILA AYE

For Maxie and for Minnie,
for Missie and for Maide.

I've signed for Cat. I've signed for Matt.
I've signed for Buzz and Belle,

For Bibi and for C.C,
for Jay and Kay and Elle.

I've signed for boys called *Romeo*
and girls called *Juliet*.

I've signed for Roman, Saxon, Dane –
though not for Norman yet.

I've signed for Raine and Breeze and Storm,
for Rainbow and for Sunny,

For Kitty and for Scottie,
for Chickie and for Bunny.

I've signed for Bear and Badger,
for Robin and for Wren,

For Zachary and Zebedee,
for Zinzan and for Zen.

Roses

I've signed for Rose and Poppy,
for Daisy and for Lily,

For Kale and Avocado,
for Pepper and for Chilli.

I've signed for Ben and Nevis,
I've signed for Star and Sky,

I've signed for April, May and June
but never for July.

I've signed for Maggie Christmas,
I've signed for Valentine,
For Holly and for Ivy,
For Bramble and for Vine.

I've signed for Fern and Forest,
for Misty, Dawn and Dew.

I've never signed for Kanga,
but once I signed for Roo.

I've signed for Peach and Clementine,
for Apple and for Cherry,

For Natty and for Tatty,
for Bonny, Blythe and Merry,

For Nixi and for Pixie,
for Fairy and for Fluff,

For Dolly and for Teddy,
for Billy and for Gruff.

I've signed for Lake and Ocean,
for Sandy and for Shelley,

For Honey and Vanilla,
and even once for Jelly.

I've signed for Scarlett, Grey and Brown,
and Violet and Blue,

And if we ever get to meet . . .

I'll sign a book for *you!*

I hope you've found some names
you didn't know about before,
And if you turn the page,
you're going to find a whole lot more!

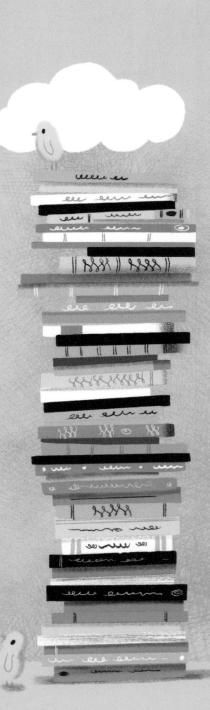

For all the children whose books I've signed
– J.D.

For Liliana and Tom
– N.A.

First published 2023 by Macmillan Children's Books
an imprint of Pan Macmillan
The Smithson, 6 Briset Street, London, EC1M 5NR
EU representative: Macmillan Publishers Ireland Limited,
1st Floor, The Liffey Trust Centre, 117-126 Sheriff Street Upper,
Dublin 1, D01 YC43
Associated companies throughout the world
www.panmacmillan.com

HB ISBN: 978-1-5290-7643-1

Text copyright © Julia Donaldson 2023
Illustrations copyright © Nila Aye 2023
Moral rights asserted.

1 3 5 7 9 8 6 4 2

A CIP catalogue record for this book is available from the British Library.

Printed in Spain

FSC
www.fsc.org

MIX
Paper from
responsible sources
FSC® C116313

maya Kimberley Kimmy Kimora Kinan Kingsley Kinny Kinty Kinvara Kiraz Kiri Kiriana Kirin
rsten Kirstie Kit Kiturah Kizzy Klara Klaudia Knox Koa Kobe Roben Koby Kodi Koen Kofi Kohana
hi Koji Kojo Konstantinos Kora Korben Korey Korina Koshi Kostas Kotaro Kotetsu Koturo Kresley
ish Krishan Krishna Krispin Krista Kristabel Kristian Kristin Kristopher Krystal Kuba Kurtis
jan Kye Kyle Kylee Kyna Kyoko Kyra Kyrav Kyrie Kyron La'Trai Lachlan Lacy Laelia Laetitia
ahaina Laia Laily Laina Laird Laissa Laith Lakita Lakshmi Lalli Lamara Lamise Lana Lander
ni Laoise Lara Laren Larichia Larissa Larkin Lars Laudika Laura Laurel Laurella Lauren
aurence Laurie Lauryn Lavender Lavinia Lawrence Lawson Lawton Layan Layla Layne Layth
azarus Lea Leah Leander Leandro Leanne Leda Lee Leela Leelou Leena Leia Leif Leigh
eighton Leila Leilani Leisha Leith Leiza Leland Lellah Lemoni Lena Leni Lenix Lenka
ennart Lennon Lennox Lenny Lentil Leo Leolin Leon Leona Leonardo Leonidas Leonie Leonne
eonor Leor Lesley Letionic Letty Lev Levi Lewis Lewmini Lex Lexie Leyland Lia Liam Lian Liana
anna Libby Liberty Lieselotte Lilan Lili Liliana Liliane Lilias Lilini Lilith Lilla Lillia Lillian
llibette Lilwen Lilya Lina Lina Lincoln Linda Lindan Lindsay Lindy Line Link Linnea Linus Lirit
s Lisa Lissy Liv Livia Livinia Livvy Liz Liza Lizanne Llew Llion Lloyd Lochan Lochie Lochy Logan
gie Loie Lois Loki Lol Lola Lolly Lolo London Lonneke Lorca Lorelei Lorena Lorenza Lorenzo
organ Lori Lorien Loris Lorne Lory Lotta Lottie Lotus Lou Louie Louis Louisa Louise Louka
ula Loulou Lourdes Louvinia Loveday Loveheart Lowell Lowenna Lowri Lua Luc Lucan Lucas
cca Lucia Lucian Luciana Luciano Lucias Lucien Lucille Lucinda Lucius Lucy Lucymarie Ludo
dovica Ludvig Luella Luis Luise Luke Lula Lulu Luma Luna Lundy Luqman Luther Lux Lyall
janna Lydia Lyle Lyndon Lyndsey Lynelle Lynette Lynn Lyra Lysander Mabel Mabon Mac
acca Macey MacKayla Mackena Mackenzie Mackie Macsen Maddison Maddox Maddy
adeleine Madelie Mae Maeby Maeline Maeryn Maeva Maeve Mafalda Magdalena Magnus
ags Maha Mahalia Mahdi Mahealani Mahi Mahira Maia Maida Maidie Maila Mair Maira Mairi
airin Maisie Maison Maite Makaveli Makena Makoto Mala Malachi Malaika Malak Malaya
alcolm Malena Mali Maliana Malik Maliki Malini Mallory Malvina Mamie Mamish Mandy
anny Manon Manraj Manu Manuel Manus Maple Mara Marc Marceline Marcia Marcie Marco
arcos Marcus Mare Mared Mareike Marek Maren Margaret Margarita Margi Margot
argueritte Maria Mariam Mariama Mariana Marianna Marianne Marie Mariella Mariette
arilyn Marin Marina Mario Marion Maris Marissa Marit Marius Mark Markos Marla Marlena
arlene Marley Marlia Marlo Marlon Marlow Marna Marnie Marsali Marshal Marta Martha
artin Marty Martyna Marv Mary Mary-Jane Marylou Marys Marysia Marzio Masha Mason
assimo Mata Mateen Matey Matheus Mathilde Matilda Mattaya Matthew Matty Matu
aud Maura Maureen Maurice Mauro Maven Maverick Mavia Max Maxim Maxime Maximilian
aximiliano Maximus Maxine Maxwell Maya Mayan Mayara Mazzie Mayzie Mea Meadow Meda
edbh Medina Meera Meesha Meg Megan Meggie Megsie Mehdi Mei Meika Meinwen Melaina
elek Melia Melina Melisa Melissa Melody Melsa Melys Meme Mena Menia Menno Mercedes
ercia Meredith Merle Merlin Merryn Meryem Meryl Mexi Mhairi Mia Miaotong Mica Michael
ichaela Michalina Michelle Mido Mieke Mihali Mikako Mike Mikenna Mikey Miki Miko Mila Milan
ilani Milda Milena Miley Militsa Milla Millan Miller Millicent Millie Milner Milo Mim Mimi Mina
indy Minky Minti Mio Mionie Miou Mira Mirabelle Miracle Miraj Miranda Mireille Mirella Miri
iriam Mirin Mirissa Miro Misa Misan Misha Mishita Mitchell Mitchum Mitty Mitzi Mizuki Mo
oana Moby Mocca Mohammed Mohira Moira Molly Momo Momoka Momu Mona Mondy Monica

Monroe Montgomery Monty Mora Moray Morgan Morgane Morna Morty Morven Morwen Mo
Mostyn Mousey Moussa Moya Mozart Mufaddal Muireann Mungo Munira Munro Murdo Murph
Murray Murrin Musa Mustafa Mveledzandivho Mya Myaan Mylee Mylene Myles Myrna Naam
Nabil Nadeem Nadia Nadine Naima Naina Nairne Nala Namaste Nana Nancy Naomi Nar
Narcisa Nash Nastassia Nat Natalia Natalie Natasha Nate Nathan Nathaniel Nava Nawe
Nayana Nazanina Nazmin Nealagh Ned Nedley Neela Neesha Neeva Nefeli Neha Nel Nelar
Nella Nelly Neo Nerea Nerin Nerys Nessa Nesta Nethuni Netta Neva Newlin Newton Ngaio Ni
Niall Niamh Nica Nicholas Nick Nicky Nico Nicola Nicole Nicoletta Niels Nigel Nihaal Nika Nik
Nikita Nikko Nile Nils Nimi Nimrod Nina Nini Niomi Nirav Nirvana Nitara Nixon Nkando NKunzie No
Noah Noe Noel Noelle Noey-Joey Nola Nona Noor Noora Nora Norea Noriki Nou Nova Novak Nov
Nua Nuala Nugget Nuno Nuria Nusaiba Nuwair Nya Nydia Nye Nyla Nyree Oak Oakley Oberys O
Ochre Octavia Odette Odh Odin Og Okalani Oksana Ola Olan Olek Olela Olina Olive Olive
Olivia Olivier Ollie Olwen Olympia Omaira Omar Omari Ona Onye Oonagh Oonash Opheli
Oran Orella Orestis Ori Oriana Orin Orion Orla Orlaith Orlanda Orlando Orly Ornella Ororoja
Orpheus Orsa Orson Osagie Oscar Osho Osian Osman Ostara Oswald Oswyn Otis Ottie Otti
Ottille Otto Ovlar Owen Owena Owethu Oz Ozil Ozzie Pablo Paddy Padma Pádraig Paige Pail
Paisley Paladin Paloma Pamela Pancho Panda Panos Paradise Param Pareesa Paris Parker Parr
Parveen Parvi Pasha Pashmina Patch Patrick Patsy Paul Paula Paulina Pavan Pavel Payson Payto
Pea Pearson Pebble Pedro Peggy Penelope Penny Penri Peony Pepe Peppercorn Percy Perdy Peregrin
Pererin Perran Perry Persephone Perseus Peta Petchnapa Pete Peter Petra Petronila Peyto
Phaedra Pharis Phil Philareti Philine Philip Philippa Phineas Phoebe Phoenix Pia Pickle Pico Pie
Pierce Piero Pierre Piers Pietro Pilar Pip Piper Pippa Pippi Piran Pitufa Pola Polina Polly Pollyann
Pom Portia Posy Prentice Presley Preston Primrose Priya Priyanka Prosper Prudence Ptolemy Pur
Puspa Qamar QinYan Qiwei Quaid Quas Quentin Quincy Quinlin Quinn Quinncess Quint Quinto
Raabia Rach Rachel Radley Radvile Rae Raelan Rafa Rafe Raff Rafferty Raffi Raghaf Rahir
Rahima Raiden Raika Raina Rainie Rajan Ralph Ralphie Ramin Ramona Ramsay Ran Ran
Rania Ranulf Raoul Raphael Raphaella Rapharoo Rasmus Ravi Rawden Raya Rayan Rayhann
Raymond Razaa Reagan Rebecca Red Redford Reece Reed Reef Reesa Reeva Reeve Reg Rega
Reggie Regina Rehan Reid Reilly Reiltin Rella Remi Remington Remo Remus Ren Renata Renr
Renuka Renzo Resa Reuben Rex Rhadija Rhea Rhiannon Rhionna Rhona Rhoslyn Rhu Rhuraid
Rhys Ria Riaan Riccardo Rich Richard Ricou Ridgeley Ridley Rihanna Riley Rio Riona Ripley Ris
Rishi Rita Ritchie Ritika Ritz River Riyad Ro Roam Roan Robbie Roben Robert Roberta Robert
Robin Robson Robyn Rocco Rochelle Rocket Rockley Rocky Roddy Rodman Rodrigo Rogan Roge
Rohan Roisin Roka Rolyn Roma Romario Romilly Romy Ron Rona Ronan Ronda Ronin Ronn
Ronwyn Ronya Rory Ros Rosa Rosabella Rosalia Rosalie Rosalind Rosalyn Rosanna Roscoe Ros
Roselyn Rosemary Rosenwyn Rosha Roshan Rosie Rosiebella Rosita Ross Rossa Rossano Roua Rou
Rowan Rowanna Rowanne Rowena Rowenna Rowland Roxanna Roxanne Roxby Roxie Roy Roy
Rozzie Ru Rubens Rudi Rudraveer Rue Rufus Rui Ruky Rumaysa Rumer Rumi Runa Rupert Russe
Ruth Ruthlyn Ry Ryan Ryder Saachi Saad Sabina Sabryna Sachelle Sachin Sade Sadie Sad
Saeed Safa Saffron Safina Safiya Saga Sage Sahara Sahib Sai Sakura Salaar Sally Salm
Salsabeel Salvador Sam Sama Saman Samantha Samara Sameer Samerell Samir
Sammy Sampuran Samson Samuel Sanaa Sango Sanjana Santiago Santino Saphira Sapph
Sara Sarah Saria Sarina Sas Sasha Saskia Sassoun Sassy Sati Satine Saul Sav Savanna